INTERIM SITE

JAI

who owns The sun?

~written & illustrated by~

STACY CHBOSKY

LANDMARK EDITIONS, INC.

P.O. Box 4469   •   1402 Kansas Avenue   •   Kansas City, Missouri 64127
(816) 241-4919

Dedicated to

Connie Bradley, William White, Dee Fazio,
and all my friends at school and the dance studio;
and to my parents, Lea and Fred Chbosky,
and my brother Stephen.
Without their encouragement and help,
I would not have been able to finish this book.

Fifth Printing

COPYRIGHT© 1988 BY STACY CHBOSKY

International Standard Book Number: 0-933849-14-1 (LIB.BDG.)

Library of Congress Cataloging-in-Publication Data
Chbosky, Stacy, 1972-
    Who owns the sun?
    Summary: Having learned from the father he admires so much that the world is filled
with things too special for any one person to own, a boy is upset to hear that he and his
father are owned by the man in the big house where they work.
    [1. Slavery — Fiction.   2. Fathers and sons — Fiction.]
I. Title.
PZ7.C3973Wh   1988   [E]   88-12694

Editorial Coordinator: Nancy R. Thatch
Creative Coordinator: David Melton
Production Assistant: Dav Pilkey

Landmark Editions, Inc.
P.O. Box 4469
1402 Kansas Avenue
Kansas City, Missouri 64127
(816) 241-4919

Printed in the United States of America

WHO OWNS THE SUN?

Every year the ten finalists in each of the three age categories of THE NATIONAL WRITTEN & ILLUSTRATED BY... AWARDS CONTEST FOR STUDENTS are so outstanding that we would be pleased to publish any of them. Therefore, we are always confident that the three top winning books selected by our judges are the *crème de la crème*.

There is no doubt WHO OWNS THE SUN? touched the minds and hearts of our judges in an extraordinary way. Stacy's beautifully written narrative transforms prose into poetry, and her impressionistic illustrations create a complete atmosphere of time and place. Her deeply moving story touches an essential part of the enduring human spirit and offers an experience, rich in texture and poignant in its plea for freedom.

At Landmark, we have been privileged to observe the development and culmination of this remarkable book. We have enjoyed working with Stacy, and we are pleased to introduce her talents as a writer and an artist in print.

We proudly present a rewarding literary experience to those who will share the delicacy of the book's poetic fiber and the power of its emotional impact.

—David Melton

Creative Coordinator
Landmark Editions, Inc.

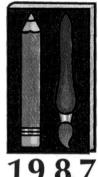

WINNER

1987
WRITTEN &
ILLUSTRATED
BY... AWARD

It was an April afternoon, and my world, now touched by the rays of the sun, smelled sweet. The light that fell across my face felt warm and clean.

"Who," I asked my father, "owns the sun?"

He pointed toward the sky and told me to look up. I raised my head and squinted my eyes against the sun's powerful glare.

"Only a fool believes he can own the sun," my father said. "Everybody sees the sun's light, and everybody feels the sun's warmth. But the sun is too large, too great, for one person to own. So it shines on all the earth and gives itself to every living thing."

I thought of what my father had said, and I believed him. I watched him as he walked away from me and went back to his work in the field.

That night we sat on the porch, resting after our day's work, and let the soft night sounds come to us. Somewhere, buried in the deep, wet grass, a cricket cried to itself. Now and then, a breeze rustled the green leaves and stirred a night lullaby.

The black sky wrapped around us like a soft muffler. The peaceful stars glowed clean white and comforted me. I leaned back in my chair for a better look at them.

"Who," I asked my father, "owns the stars?"

"The stars are too far away to be owned by anyone," my father answered quietly. "No one has ever touched the stars, but everyone looks at them, and everyone wonders at their beauty. The stars light the night sky and shine for all people to see."

Time passed, and spring gave way to summer. The rays of the hot sun burned deep into the ground.

In late July, a welcome rain fell onto the earth and began to heal the scars the sun had left behind. The thirsty ground that lay cracked in dusty spirals drank deeply and once again became a rich, dark brown.

"Who," I asked my father, "owns the rain?"

"No one owns the rain," my father told me, as he scooped up a handful of moist dirt and let the soil sprinkle through his fingers.

"The rain gives life to this earth," he said.

"Sometimes rain can be too strong and flood the land," my father explained. "It can also be gentle and nourish seeds in the ground. But the rain cannot be owned by anyone. It gives freely of itself and falls on every land in the world."

The next day, after the rain had stopped, the air again grew still and hot. It was heavy and thick, and it seemed to smother everything it touched. It pressed on my chest and made me long for a deep breath of fresh air.

I stayed inside most of the day, hoping for a cool breeze. Just before dinner, it came. First there was a gentle stirring of wind. Then soft breezes blew and began to push the hot air away. I filled my lungs and let the air cool my whole body. It was a wonderful feeling.

"Who," I asked my father, "owns the wind?"

"No one," my father answered, as he turned to face the breeze. "The wind is too mighty to be owned by anyone. Sometimes the wind is moody and shows its evil temper. It whirls into a storm and crushes everything in its path. Or the wind can be funny and blow the hat off your head. Or it can turn a windmill and help a man do his work. And sometimes it can be pleasant and cool, just like it is right now.

"But no one owns the wind," my father said. "It roams the earth. It is a wanderer that visits everyone and every place."

The next morning, I awoke to the fragrance of my mother's biscuits baking in the oven. The smell made me hungry, so I dressed quickly and joined my father at the breakfast table.

From far away, I heard the clear, sweet trill of a bird's call. A second bird answered with a stream of chirps. While we ate, the birds continued their friendly greetings.

"Who," I asked my father, "owns the birds?"

"Nobody can own the birds," my father answered. "Everyone hears them sing their songs, and everyone watches them soar and glide across the sky. But birds can fly away at any time and go anywhere they choose. They are too free to be owned, but they share their beauty and their songs with the whole world."

There were wildflowers growing in the field behind our house. They brightened the summer with colorful beauty. There were lavender ones, orange ones, and yellow ones with golden edges. But my favorites were the pink ones that bloomed in the clearest, softest shade of rose I had ever seen.

The flowers appeared so peaceful and at home in their beds. Only in midsummer, when the world was overflowing with flowers, would I allow myself to pick a small bouquet for my mother's table. When placed in a jar of water, the flowers looked so lovely, and their fragrance filled the house.

"Who," I asked my father, "owns the flowers?"

"A man can pick any flowers he chooses," my father answered, "but the flowers belong to the land. The land was here long before man, and it will be here after he is gone.

"Flowers give their beauty for all people to enjoy," my father said. "If we don't destroy the flowers, they will bloom and seed, and more flowers will grow in their place."

I did not understand all my father had said, but I accepted it. He had told me the world was full of beautiful things — things that could not be owned, but that could be loved and appreciated by everyone.

I knew my father was a great man. He had a strong body and a kind heart. His huge hands were cracked and weathered by the sun and calloused from his work. And yet, when he put his hands over mine, they felt as warm and gentle as my mother's. My own hands were small and soft, making his even more fascinating to me. I hoped that one day I would have hands that were as strong and gentle as his.

I was not the only one who had respect for my father. I noticed the way other men watched him as he worked. I knew how they sometimes counted on him for help.

The men called my father "Big Jim," which certainly described him, because he was taller and stronger than any of them. When he bent over the plow and dug it into the earth, his muscles strained and pressed hard against the cloth of his shirt.

My father was so tall that I had to lean my head way back to look into his eyes. But when our eyes finally met, there was always a smile on his face — a smile just for me, his firstborn son.

My mother cooked in the big house for Mr. Finley and his family. Every day about noon, I would go to the huge kitchen and breathe in the hot, steamy smells of pies and cookies baking. My mother would fill a pail with meat, beans and biscuits, and sometimes a piece of pie for my father's lunch. And she would fill a jug with cool buttermilk.

Carrying the pail and jug, I'd run to my father who was working in the field. My errand was a labor of love. I ran because I loved my father and because I knew how hungry and thirsty he would be. Across the fields I'd race, never slowing my pace or stopping to look around.

But, one day...it was late in August, as I recall...the day was so hot and the air so heavy that I slowed down and walked part of the way. As I came to the west field, I heard the sounds of men talking. When I drew near, I recognized Mr. Finley, the owner of the big house, and saw another man who was a stranger to me.

"See that big fella over there?" I heard Mr. Finley say as he leaned against the fence. "That's Big Jim. He's a strong one, that man."

I realized Mr. Finley was referring to my father, so I slowed my pace even more. And when the stranger said, "Just look at him lift those rocks!" I could not help but feel proud.

"He's our best field hand, all right," Mr. Finley said. "Why, he'll have all the rocks out of that field by the end of the week."

"I wish I had him working in my fields," the other man said.

"Yes, Big Jim puts all other field hands to shame," Mr. Finley agreed, lighting his cigar and blowing a puff of blue smoke into the air. "I wish I owned ten more just like him."

For a moment, I just stood there. I could not believe my ears. Mr. Finley's words echoed in my mind — "I wish I owned ten more just like him."

Owned! How could that be? It couldn't be true! Suddenly, I did not want to hear more. And I didn't want to think about what I had just heard, but I couldn't help myself.

I climbed over the fence and ran across the field. The lunch pail banged against my leg and buttermilk sloshed from the jug, but I didn't care.

When my father saw me approaching, he stood up straight, smiled and waved to me as he usually did. But when he saw how upset I was, the smile quickly disappeared from his face. I didn't stop running until I was standing squarely in front of him.

"I just heard Mr. Finley say he **owned** you," I blurted out. "Is that true?" I asked.

My father's face tightened with anger and pain. His hands clenched into fists, the muscles of his arms suddenly swelled, and then he turned away.

"Does Mr. Finley own you?" I asked again.

Finally, my father turned back to me. It was when I saw the sadness on his face that I knew — the words Mr. Finley had spoken were true.

"But he doesn't own the stars or the sun," I reasoned. "So how can he own you?"

My father was quiet for what seemed a long time. Finally, he spoke.

"A man is a beautiful thing," he said, "a very beautiful thing. But some men forget this. And sometimes they try to keep other men captive. They buy and sell people, as if human beings are no more than cattle.

"But only a fool believes he can really own another man, and only a fool will try," my father said. "Mr. Finley may own my body, but I have a heart and I have a mind, and he can never own these. Inside of me, I'm too powerful to be owned by anyone. Inside, I am like the sun."

I listened to the words my father spoke. I considered them carefully, trying to sort out the thoughts that raced through my mind. Finally, I settled on the one question I knew I had to ask —

"Does Mr. Finley own me too?" I wanted to know.

My father looked directly into my eyes for a moment, and for a moment after that. He bent down and put his arms around me, and then he began to cry.

Afterword

Looking back, I think my childhood was ended that summer day. Many cold winters lay ahead.

In his lifetime, my father saw many changes. He lived to stand at last as a free man and to see his children attend school. One of my brothers became a musician, the other one is a Baptist minister. My sister opened a restaurant, and I became a teacher.

My parents hoped and dreamed that the time would come when our people would not be judged by the color of their skins, but would be respected for the quality of their thoughts and deeds. I am sure my parents would have been pleased — no, overjoyed — if they could have known that one of their great grandchildren would one day be elected governor of our state.

BOOKS FOR STUDENTS
– WINNERS OF THE NATIONAL WRITTEN &

una Chandrasekhar
age 9

Anika Thomas
age 13

Cara Reichel
age 15

Jonathan Kahn
age 9

Adam Moore
age 9

slie Ann MacKeen
age 9

Elizabeth Haidle
age 13

Amy Hagstrom
age 9

Isaac Whitlatch
age 11

Dav Pilkey
age 19

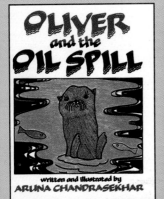

by Aruna Chandrasekhar, age 9
Houston, Texas

A touching and timely story! When the lives of many otters are threatened by a huge oil spill, a group of concerned people come to their rescue. Wonderful illustrations.
Printed Full Color
ISBN 0-933849-33-8

by Anika D. Thomas, age 13
Pittsburgh, Pennsylvania

A compelling autobiography! A young girl's heartrending account of growing up in a tough, inner-city neighborhood. The illustrations match the mood of this gripping story.
Printed Two Colors
ISBN 0-933849-34-6

by Cara Reichel, age 15
Rome, Georgia

Elegant and eloquent! A young stonecutter vows to create a great statue for his impoverished village. But his fame almost stops him from fulfilling that promise.
Printed Two Colors
ISBN 0-933849-35-4

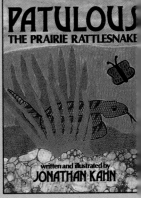

by Jonathan Kahn, age 9
Richmond Heights, Ohio

A fascinating nature story! Wh Patulous, a prairie rattlesna searches for food, he must try avoid the claws and fangs of his o enemies.
Printed Full Color
ISBN 0-933849-36-2

by Adam Moore, age 9
Broken Arrow, Oklahoma

A remarkable true story! When Adam was eight years old, he fell and ran an arrow into his head. With rare insight and humor, he tells of his ordeal and his amazing recovery.
Printed Two Colors
ISBN 0-933849-24-9

by Michael Aushenker, age 19
Ithaca, New York

Chomp! Chomp! When Arthur forgets to feed his goat, the animal eats everything in sight. A very funny story — good to the last bite. The illustrations are terrific.
Printed Full Color
ISBN 0-933849-28-1

by Leslie Ann MacKeen, age 9
Winston-Salem, North Carolina

Loaded with fun and puns! When Jeremiah T. Fitz's car stops running, several animals offer suggestions for fixing it. The results are hilarious. The illustrations are charming.
Printed Full Color
ISBN 0-933849-19-2

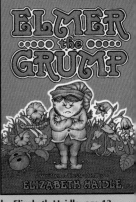

by Elizabeth Haidle, age 13
Beaverton, Oregon

A very touching story! The gru iest Elfkin learns to cherish friendship of others after he h an injured snail and befriends orphaned boy. Absolutely beauti
Printed Full Color
ISBN 0-933849-20-6

by Amy Hagstrom, age 9
Portola, California

An exciting western! When a boy and an old Indian try to save a herd of wild ponies, they discover a lost canyon and see the mystical vision of the Great White Stallion.
Printed Full Color
ISBN 0-933849-15-X

by Isaac Whitlatch, age 11
Casper, Wyoming

The true confessions of a devout vegetable hater! Isaac tells ways to avoid and dispose of the "slimy green things." His colorful illustrations provide a salad of laughter and mirth.
Printed Full Color
ISBN 0-933849-16-8

by Dav Pilkey, age 19
Cleveland, Ohio

A thought-provoking parable! Two kings halt an arms race and learn to live in peace. This outstanding book launched Dav's career. He now has seven more books published.
Printed Full Color
ISBN 0-933849-22-2

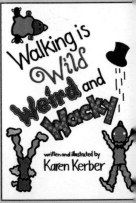

by Karen Kerber, age 12
St. Louis, Missouri

A delightfully playful book! The is loaded with clever alliterations gentle humor. Karen's brightly ored illustrations are compose wiggly and waggly strokes of ge
Printed Full Color
ISBN 0-933849-29-X

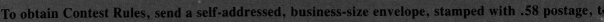
To obtain Contest Rules, send a self-addressed, business-size envelope, stamped with .58 postage, t

BY STUDENTS!

ILLUSTRATED BY . . . AWARDS FOR STUDENTS –

by Jayna Miller, age 19
Zanesville, Ohio

he funniest Halloween ever! When mmer the Rabbit takes all the eats, his friends get even. Their ilarious scheme includes a haunted ouse and mounds of chocolate.
inted Full Color
BN 0-933849-37-0

Jayna Miller
age 19

by Lauren Peters, age 7
Kansas City, Missouri

The Christmas that almost wasn't! When Santa Claus takes a vacation, Mrs. Claus and the elves go on strike. Toys aren't made. Cookies aren't baked. Super illustrations.
Printed Full Color
ISBN 0-933849-25-7

Lauren Peters
age 7

by Michael Cain, age 11
Annapolis, Maryland

A glorious tale of adventure! To become a knight, a young man must face a beast in the forest, a spell-binding witch, and a giant bird that guards a magic oval crystal.
Printed Full Color
ISBN 0-933849-26-5

Michael Cain
age 11

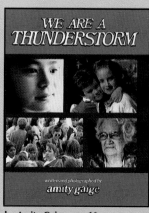

by Amity Gaige, age 16
Reading, Pennsylvania

A lyrical blend of poetry and pho-tographs! Amity's sensitive poems offer thought-provoking ideas and amusing insights. This lovely book is one to be savored and enjoyed.
Printed Full Color
ISBN 0-933849-27-3

Heidi Salter
age 19

Heidi Salter, age 19
Berkeley, California

pooky and wonderful! To save her vid imagination, a young girl must onfront the Great Grey Grimly mself. The narrative is filled with spense. Vibrant illustrations.
inted Full Color
BN 0-933849-21-4

Amity Gaige
age 16

by Dennis Vollmer, age 6
Grove, Oklahoma

A baby whale's curiosity gets him into a lot of trouble. GUINNESS BOOK OF RECORDS lists Dennis as the youngest author/illustrator of a published book.
Printed Full Color
ISBN 0-933849-12-5

Dennis Vollmer
age 6

by Lisa Gross, age 12
Santa Fe, New Mexico

A touching story of self-esteem! A puppy is laughed at because of his unusual appearance. His search for acceptance is told with sensitivity and humor. Wonderful illustrations.
Printed Full Color
ISBN 0-933849-13-3

Lisa Gross
age 12

by Stacy Chbosky, age 14
Pittsburgh, Pennsylvania

A powerful plea for freedom! This emotion-packed story of a young slave touches an essential part of the human spirit. Made into a film by Disney Educational Productions.
Printed Full Color
ISBN 0-933849-14-1

Stacy Chbosky
age 14

David McAdoo, age 14
Springfield, Missouri

n exciting intergalactic adventure! the distant future, a courageous rrior defends a kingdom from a agon from outer space. Astound-g sepia illustrations.
nted Duotone
3N 0-933849-23-0

Karen Kerber
age 12

by Bonnie-Alise Leggat, age 8
Culpeper, Virginia

Amy J. Kendrick wants to play foot-ball, but her mother wants her to become a ballerina. Their clash of wills creates hilarious situations. Clever, delightful illustrations!
Printed Full Color
ISBN 0-933849-39-7

by Lisa Kirsten Butenhoff, age 13
Woodbury, Minnesota

The people of a Russian village face the winter without warm clothes or enough food. Then their lives are improved by a young girl's gifts. A tender story with lovely illustrations.
Printed Full Color
ISBN 0-933849-40-0

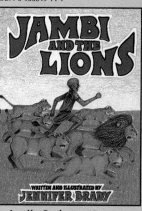

by Jennifer Brady, age 17
Columbia, Missouri

When poachers capture a pride of lions, a native boy tries to free the animals. A skillfully told story. Glowing illustrations illuminate this African adventure.
Printed Full Color
ISBN 0-933849-41-9

David McAdoo
age 14

CONTEST FOR STUDENTS, Landmark Editions, Inc., P.O. Box 4469, Kansas City, MO 64127.